WIN A NAUGHTY FAIRIES T-SHIRT!

Every time those Naughty Fairies
are hatching a plan they do their fairy code
where they come up with NF words...

Niggle Flaptart
Nicely Framed
Nimble Fingers

Can you help the Naughty Fairies
find two more words beginning with
N.................. and F...................?

Each month we will select the best entries to win a very
special Naughty Fairies T-shirt and they will go into the
draw to have their NF idea printed in the next lot of books!

Don't forget to include your name and address.
Send your entry to: Naughty Fairies NF Competition,
Hodder Children's Marketing, 338 Euston Road,
London NW1 3BH.
Australian readers should write to:
Hachette Children's Books, Level 17/207 Kent Street,
Sydney, NSW 2000

For Terms and Conditions: www.hachettechildrens.co.uk/terms

An Utter Flutter

Lucy Mayflower

Hodder
Children's
Books

A division of Hachette Children's Books

Special thanks to Lucy Courtenay

Created by Hodder Children's Books and Lucy Courtenay
Text and illustrations copyright © 2007 Hodder Children's Books
Illustrations created by Artful Doodlers

First published in Great Britain in 2007
by Hodder Children's Books

1

A Catalogue record for this book is available from the British Library

ISBN – 10: 0 340 94429 3
ISBN – 13: 978 0 340 94429 5

Printed in the UK by CPI Bookmarque, Croydon, CR0 4TD

The paper and board used in this paperback by Hodder Children's Books are natural recyclable products made from wood grown in sustainable forests. The manufacturing processes conform to the environmental regulations of the country of origin.

Hodder Children's Books
A division of Hachette Children's Books
338 Euston Rd, London NW1 3BH

Contents

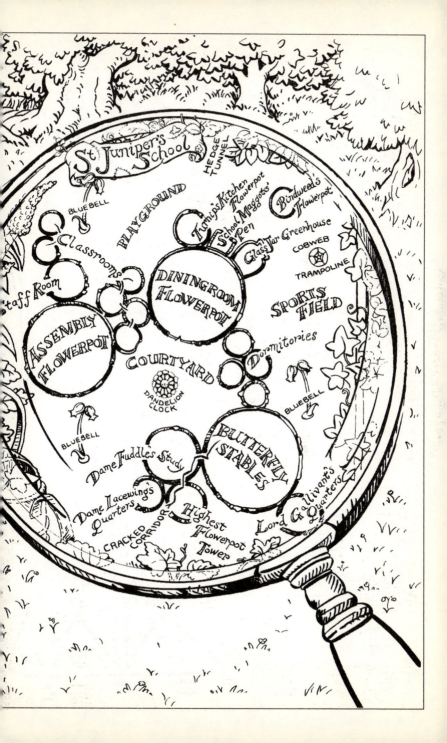

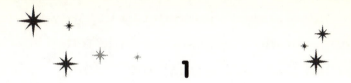

1

Flutterball

Down at the bottom of the garden, a thistle seed floated peacefully in the air above the St Juniper's Sports Field.

"FLUTTERBALL!" roared a tall blond elf sitting astride a Red Admiral butterfly. He blew a slim twig whistle.

"FLUTTERBALL!" twenty-three fairies roared back. The seed disappeared in a whirl of brightly coloured butterfly wings and even more brightly coloured language.

"Out of the way, fatso . . ."

"Hey! Get off!"

"Mine! It's MINE!"

"Lord Gallivant! Kelpie pulled my wings . . ."

"You shouldn't have got in the way then, should you?" shouted the red-haired fairy riding a fat and puffing bumblebee towards the thistle seed. "Flap, Flea! *Flap!*"

The bumblebee whizzed its stumpy wings as fast as it could. Untouched by the breeze, the thistle seed started sinking to the ground.

"Get off that bumblebee, Kelpie!" shouted the elf. "Where is the butterfly I put you on?"

Kelpie kicked Flea towards the thistle seed again. "I lost it, Lord Gallivant!" she shouted back.

"Lost it?" Lord Gallivant thundered. "How did you lose it?"

"Losing butterflies is easy," Kelpie yelled. "You just climb off and let go."

Flea the bumblebee made one last effort to flap the thistle seed into the air.

"Forget it, Kelpie!" called a spiky-haired fairy zooming high above the game on a huge blue dragonfly. "Bumblebees are rubbish at flutterball. Leave it to me and Pong!"

"Get off Pong this instant, Ping!" roared Lord Gallivant. He was beginning to turn purple. "It's against the rules! Dragonflies and bumblebees can't play flutterball, their wings are the wrong size— hey! Hey, you! Stop that!"

Lord Gallivant hurried off to the far side of the flutterball game, where four fairies had started a fight.

A pretty curly-haired fairy on a Large White butterfly swooped down to a blonde fairy on a Tortoiseshell. "I don't think Lord Gallivant likes flutterball practice much," she said, hovering expertly on the breeze. "What do you think, Nettle?"

They watched as the butterfly-riding teacher tried to separate the fighting fairies. A fairy fist lashed out and whacked Lord Gallivant on the ear.

"I think," said Nettle, "that you are right, Brilliance."

Flutterball was not a dainty sport. Flapping a thistle seed up and down a pitch using nothing but the wind from a butterfly's wings, and scoring goals by fluttering the seed into flowers, was only half of it. Fairy players had to barge each other out of the way, fly upside down without falling off, never take their eyes off the thistle seed for an instant and never, EVER, touch the seed. If the seed hit the ground instead of a flower, the game had to start again. If the seed hit a fairy or a butterfly, the game also had to start again. If a fairy hit another fairy or a referee – well. That was just tough.

The thistle seed was now floating dangerously close to the ground. Two little fairies, one on a Meadow Blue and the other on a magnificent Brimstone, whooped and zoomed beneath the seed to stop it landing on the grass.

"Hey!" said Brilliance, standing up on her butterfly's back to get a better view. "Look at Tiptoe!"

Tiptoe, on the Meadow Blue butterfly, had managed to push the thistle seed back into the air without touching it. The Brimstone-riding fairy now scooped up the seed with the draught from her butterfly's wings and fluttered it expertly towards a daisy.

"Good one, Sesame!" Brilliance called. "Go, Tiptoe!"

Tiptoe, Sesame and their butterflies worked together to flutter the thistle seed into the heart of the daisy. When it landed, everyone cheered – except for the fighting fairies, who were still fighting, and Lord Gallivant, who was now wailing, hopping around and clutching his shin.

"Brilliant!" Brilliance sang.

Beside her, Nettle punched the air and nearly fell off her Tortoiseshell. Ping and Pong performed a glittering blue loop of triumph over their heads. Kelpie clapped hard, and Flea sank exhausted down to the grass to lie in a furry panting heap with his legs in the air.

Sesame raised her hand for Tiptoe to high-five. With her other hand, she patted the neck of her Brimstone. "Fantastic fluttering, Sulphur! Extra nectar for you tonight!"

"You too, Cobalt," said Tiptoe, kissing her Meadow Blue.

The fighting fairies had stopped fighting, and were now cheerfully comparing bruises. The rest of the class dismounted and chattered among themselves.

Lying flat on his back with his hair in disarray, Lord Gallivant put the twig whistle to his lips and blew feebly. Flutterball practice was over.

*

"Flutterball always makes me hungry," said Tiptoe, helping herself to a large plate of seed bread at lunchtime.

"You were brilliant," said Brilliance. "You deserve to be in the Flutterball Final for sure this year."

The Flutterball Final was held at the midsummer new moon every year. St Juniper's and their archrivals, Ambrosia Academy, took turns to host the tournament. The fairies at St Juniper's would have liked to take turns at winning it, too. However, Ambrosia Academy had won it more times than St Juniper's liked to remember.

Tiptoe blushed at Brilliance's compliment. "Do you think so?"

"You and Sesame made a brilliant team," Brilliance said.

"Sulphur's perfect for flutterball," Sesame said proudly.

"Sulphur's perfect for most things,"

Nettle said. "He's the fastest butterfly in our stable."

"And Flea's the fastest bee," said Kelpie at once. At Kelpie's feet, Flea buzzed at the mention of his name.

"And Pong," began Ping.

"Oh shut up, both of you," said Brilliance. "Flutterball is a sport for butterflies, whether you like it or not. And with Tiptoe and Sesame on the team, perhaps we'll beat Ambrosia Academy this year."

"I'm not hopeful," said Kelpie.

"You never are," Nettle pointed out.

The Naughty Fairies sat down at their favourite bark table.

"It would be wonderful if we *could* win this year," said Sesame longingly.

"You need a team of six decent flutterball players," Ping said. "We've got two."

"You could be quite good if you tried, Kelpie," said Tiptoe. "Nettle isn't too bad, and Brilliance is—"

"Brilliant," said Brilliance modestly. "I am, aren't I."

"And if Ping tried a few of her dragonfly moves on a butterfly," Tiptoe persisted, "we could be unbeatable."

"Dream on," said Kelpie. "Ambrosia Academy get a special flutterball training coach, and their butterflies are always better than ours. St Juniper's doesn't stand a chance."

Suddenly, Tiptoe stuck out her fist. "Naughty Fairies!"

"Natural fog," said Brilliance at once, and put her fist on Tiptoe's.

Kelpie put her fist on Brilliance's. "Nonsensical fishcake."

"Nightingale fluid," added Nettle.

"I can never think of anything starting with NF!" Sesame wailed as the others looked at her. "And when I do, they're always wrong!"

"Forget it, Sesame," said Ping with a

sigh. "I'll do two. Nine flies, and ninety frogs. Fly, fly . . ."

"'To the SKY!" the other fairies chanted, and threw their hands up into the air.

"We have to try and win the Flutterball Final this year," said Tiptoe.

The Naughty Fairies groaned.

"No way . . ."

"Not a chance . . ."

"We *have* to," Tiptoe interrupted doggedly. "And you've all NFed, so you can't back out now. We've got one week until the new moon and the Flutterball Final. We should give it a try at flutterball practice tomorrow."

"I can't believe I have to ride a *butterfly*," said Kelpie in disgust. By her feet, Flea growled in disapproval. "We'd better get into the Flutterball Final after this. I've got my hedge cred to think of."

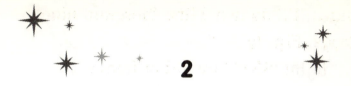

2

A Nasty Surprise

In the misty dawn light, Sesame slipped into the Butterfly Stables. She wanted to spend some time with her butterfly Sulphur before breakfast, to give him some extra nectar before flutterball practice.

Sulphur put his yellow head over his stable door and purred as Sesame stroked him.

"I do love you, Sulphur," said Sesame, laying her head against the Brimstone butterfly's furry cheek. "I loved you when you were Sprout the caterpillar, but I love you even more now. You're the best butterfly in the whole world."

Sulphur curled out his long tongue and licked at the nectar Sesame had brought. He flexed his golden wings, and Sesame felt the breeze on her skin.

"We're going to get a really good flutterball team together," Sesame promised. "Even Kelpie's going to try flying a butterfly. What do you think of that?"

Sulphur purred a bit louder.

"I know," said Sesame. "It'll give Flea a nice break from carrying Kelpie around all the time."

A soft chittering noise made Sesame turn her head. She caught sight of a Large White flying out through the stable doors, beating its black and white patterned wings. It was out of sight within moments.

"That's funny," Sesame said with a frown. "I didn't see anyone else when I came into the stables. Did you, Sulphur?"

She stared at the open door. Had she

shut it when she came in? She
wondered uneasily if the Large White
had escaped by itself.

Sulphur butted her shoulder.
Forgetting about the Large White,

Sesame turned back to her butterfly and dropped a kiss on his nose. Then she flew out of the stable and down to the Dining Flowerpot for breakfast.

Lord Gallivant stared at Kelpie. "You actually *want* a butterfly for flutterball practice today?" he repeated.

Brilliance nudged Kelpie in the back.

"Yes," Kelpie muttered, stroking Flea's head.

"And you won't lose it?" Lord Gallivant persisted.

Kelpie stroked Flea's head a bit harder. "No."

"Me too, Lord Gallivant," said Ping reluctantly. "I don't mind leaving Pong in the stable today."

Lord Gallivant mopped his forehead with a petal hankie. "You . . . don't?"

Ping bit her lip and shook her head.

"Well," said Lord Gallivant at last. "Miracles do happen. When I won the

Midsummer Champion Butterfly Race—"

A chorus of groans rose from the fairies who had gathered in the Butterfly Stables. Everyone knew about Lord Gallivant and the Midsummer Champion Butterfly Race. It was the elf's favourite subject.

"When I won the Midsummer Champion Butterfly Race," Lord Gallivant continued, raising his voice, "my butterfly had injured itself on its stable door before the race. Everyone agreed that my extraordinary win truly was a miracle." He smiled fondly at the memory.

Brilliance mimed a yawn at the others, who giggled.

"Very well," said Lord Gallivant, pulling himself back from the past with an effort. "Ping, Kelpie – you will find a pair of Small Whites called Quartz and Quince in the last stable on the left. They are both young and a little unpredictable, so be careful with them. Everyone, mount up! I'll see you on the pitch in two dandelion seeds."

"Small Whites are quite fast," said Sesame, sounding pleased as everyone rushed to find a butterfly.

"Not as fast as Pong," said Ping. She glanced at her dragonfly, who was staring disdainfully out of his stable.

"Nor as furry as Flea," said Kelpie gloomily. "He always keeps my knees nice and warm."

Flea buzzed and butted his head against Kelpie's hand.

"You both did the NF promise," Tiptoe reminded them, unhooking Cobalt's stable door.

"And Ping actually did it twice," Brilliance added.

Kelpie and Ping trailed off to the last stable on the left.

"So," said Kelpie. "Which one's Quartz, and which one's Quince?"

Leaving Kelpie and Ping to work out which butterfly was which, Brilliance peered over a nearby stable door. "That's funny," she said with a frown. "Chalky's not here." Chalky was the Large White that Brilliance had ridden at flutterball practice the day before.

Sesame remembered the Large White she had seen flying out of the stable that morning. "I think Chalky might have escaped," she said as she unstabled Sulphur. She told Brilliance what she'd seen.

"Don't worry about it," said Brilliance. "I'm brilliant at flying most butterflies. I'll just take the next one along."

The stall next to Chalky's was occupied by a very bald and tattered Cabbage White called Snowball. Snowball was the oldest butterfly in the stables. His wings were see-through and his tongue had lost its curl.

"Oh," said Brilliance doubtfully. "It's you, Snowball."

Snowball gave a croaky purr.

Brilliance glanced around. The rest of the Butterfly Stable was now empty.

"See it as a challenge for your brilliant butterfly-riding skills," Sesame suggested kindly. And she kicked Sulphur and took off at speed through the Butterfly Stable doors.

*

"You see?" said Sesame triumphantly, as they groomed their butterflies after the practice. "I told you you could be good, Kelpie."

"Hmph," said Kelpie, looking pleased. She brushed her Small White a little harder than necessary. The butterfly squeaked.

"You and Quartz saved at least four flutterball goals," Tiptoe added, straightening out one of Cobalt's wings.

"This one's Quince," said Kelpie.

"Whatever," said Tiptoe. "You and Ping made a good team at the back."

"No one was expecting my loop-the-loop," said Ping modestly.

"I knew your dragonfly moves would come in useful," said Tiptoe.

"We were all brilliant," said Brilliance. She glanced at Snowball a little sourly.

"Snowball never even got off the ground," Nettle pointed out.

"He stopped a flutterball from landing

on the grass," Brilliance insisted.

"Only because it landed on *him*," said Sesame. "Never mind, Brilliance. Chalky will be back in time for the next practice, and then there'll be no stopping you."

Brilliance looked happier.

"I wonder where Chalky is?" Nettle asked as they all flew to the Dining Flowerpot for lunch.

"Probably stuffing himself with buddleia nectar and sunbathing," said Kelpie. "There's nothing like a bit of freedom to make you feel good."

"He'll be back tonight," Tiptoe predicted. "Butterflies hate the dark."

After lunch, the fairies had Nature Studies with their favourite teacher, Dame Honey. Dame Honey was young and pretty, and always wore beautiful clothes. Today, she was dressed from top to toe in bluebell petals, with a chunky pair of cobnut clogs on her feet.

The fairies hardly ever misbehaved during Dame Honey's classes. For today's lesson, the fairies had gathered outside the school's glass-jar greenhouse. Bindweed the garden pixie was weeding the daisy beds when they arrived. As they all clattered inside, he scowled at them and retreated. Bindweed didn't like fairies much, especially after all the pranks the St Juniper's pupils had played on him in recent weeks.

"Today we are looking at diets," Dame Honey told the class as they settled down among the stems and leaves of the greenhouse.

Tiptoe looked worried at the mention of diets. So did Flea, who was halfway through a honeycake.

"Not a slimming diet," Dame Honey said. "The kind of food we eat." She tapped the bushy plant next to her.

"Does anyone know what this is?"

No one did.

"This," said Dame Honey, "is called stinking goose-foot."

The fairies giggled. Some held their noses and waved their hands in the air.

"Does it taste of stinking geese feet?" asked Sesame.

"I don't know," said Dame Honey. "I've never tasted geese feet. Goblins love it."

Dame Honey pulled off several flowers and passed them around the class, together with petal paper, splinter pencils and drawing instructions. Soon, the greenhouse was decorated with petal pictures of the stinking goose-foot, which the fairies stuck up on the curved glass walls.

The next plant they studied was called hairy spurge. It was eaten by imps, "who like to boil it up with beetle toes," according to Dame Honey. One or two fairies shrieked. Sesame, who loved beetles, turned white.

Towards the end of the lesson, Dame Honey clapped her hands for silence.

"We are looking at one last plant today," she said. "And for this, we need a little magic." She pulled out her wand and pointed it up at the sun, which was blazing through the glass roof of the greenhouse. "*Nox!*" she cried.

The greenhouse was plunged into darkness. Small sparkles of light appeared, floating in the air like tiny stars. The fairies squealed in surprise.

"As you might guess by its name," said Dame Honey, "the night-flowering catchfly flowers by night and catches flies on its sticky stems."

She indicated a little plant which was growing beside the greenhouse door. Now that everything was dark, it was putting out slim pink petals.

"Who eats that, Dame Honey?" asked Nettle with interest.

Dame Honey gave a curious smile. "Night sprites," she told the class.

The glass-jar greenhouse erupted with noise.

"Night sprites don't exist, Dame

Honey!" Ping shouted above the racket. "Everyone knows that!"

Brilliance made googly night-sprite eyes at Nettle, and they both collapsed in giggles.

"Oooh," said Kelpie. "Flittery fluttery!"

Several timid fairies screamed and hid their eyes as Kelpie jumped around the greenhouse making flittering motions with her hands.

"Be quiet, everyone!" Tiptoe shouted crossly. "Night sprites do exist! I've seen them!"

The fairies stopped rioting. Everyone turned and stared at Tiptoe.

"I have," Tiptoe insisted. "I was on detention in the Woods a couple of moons ago, and I saw them. They had green faces, and black cloaks, and they zoomed around in the moonlight. On moths!"

Even Dame Honey couldn't control the commotion which followed Tiptoe's words. As the spell faded and the sunlight returned, the night-flowering catchfly pulled its petals shut. And twenty-five over-excited fairies streamed out of the greenhouse with a dozen detentions and an armful of homework between them.

"Did you *really* see night sprites that time in the wood?" Sesame asked Tiptoe as the Naughty Fairies finished their supper and headed to the Butterfly Stables.

"For the hundredth time, yes," said Tiptoe with a sigh.

"*Really* really?" Nettle persisted.

"How many times do I have to repeat myself?" Tiptoe demanded. "I. Saw. Night. Sprites. Can we stop talking about them now? We've got flying practice to think about."

They pushed open the door to the Butterfly Stables. To their surprise, they found several weeping fairies and a very pale-faced Lord Gallivant waiting for them.

"What's happened?" Sesame asked. A lump of fear rose in her throat. "Is Sulphur OK?"

Sulphur put his furry head over the door of his stable and purred at Sesame.

"Sulphur's fine," sniffed a chubby fairy with blonde pompom bunches in her hair. "But Syrup's disappeared!"

"Pelly, that's awful!" Nettle gasped.

"Pelargonium's Meadow Brown is not the only butterfly which has gone missing," said Lord Gallivant gravely.

The Naughty Fairies flinched. Pelly usually hit anyone who called her by her full name.

Pelly, however, hadn't noticed. She rubbed her eyes. "Chalky hasn't come back yet. Ivory's gone too," she said, referring to one of the better school butterflies. "And Tiptoe? So's Cobalt!"

3

Suspicions

Flying practice that evening was very sombre. Only a few fairies were swooping overhead, practising flutterball dives. Most of the others were huddled in little groups by the ivy-covered fence, discussing the mystery of the missing butterflies.

"I think it's Ambrosia Academy," said Kelpie, stroking Flea as she sat with her back to a smooth, shiny ivy leaf. "Remember the time they kidnapped Flea and shaved his fur off so they could win that stupid Furriest Bumblebee trophy? I bet they've kidnapped our butterflies so they win the Flutterball Final next week."

"But they always win anyway," Nettle pointed out. "Why bother stealing our butterflies?"

"Because they know it will upset us," said Sesame. She put her arm around a red-eyed Tiptoe.

"Lord Gallivant thinks it's Bindweed's fault," said Ping.

On the other side of the Sports Field, Lord Gallivant was shouting something at Bindweed. It didn't look like Bindweed was listening.

"What's Bindweed got to do with it?"
asked Tiptoe.

"Lord Gallivant thinks the butterflies
have been escaping through a crack in
the stable wall," said Ping. "I heard him
talking to Bindweed earlier, when I was
feeding Pong."

"Lord Gallivant's wrong and Kelpie's
right," said Brilliance. "It's definitely
Ambrosia Academy. And I've got a
brilliant plan. Naughty Fairies!" She
put her fist down on the springy grass.

"No flying," said Tiptoe sadly, resting
her fist on Brilliance's.

"Nit fat."

"Not fit."

"Net phut."

"Nettle's friends," said Nettle. "And
by the way – phut starts with 'ph',
Sesame."

"*Stupid* spelling," Sesame grumbled.

"Fly, fly . . ."

"To the SKY!"

Brilliance grinned at her friends. "Ambrosia Academy will be practising for the Flutterball Final, same as us. Let's go and see if they've still got all their butterflies. If they have . . ."

". . . then they're definitely the butterfly thieves!" Kelpie finished triumphantly.

"We'll go and spy on them at dawn tomorrow," Brilliance said.

"You know we're not allowed away from St Juniper's without permission," said Sesame.

"When's that ever stopped us?" Kelpie said loftily.

"We can ride Pong," said Ping. "He's big enough to carry all of us the whole way to the Wood."

"Can I ride at the back, please?" Nettle asked.

Ping nodded. "Why?"

"I'm further away from his teeth," Nettle explained.

*

Kelpie was the first to wake up the next morning. Flea was licking the end of her nose, his wings tickling her chin. Outside the window, the sky was showing the palest edge of daylight.

Kelpie shook the others awake. "We've got about one dandelion before lessons," she said as everyone wriggled into their clothes. "Brilliance, are you sure the Ambrosia fairies will have butterfly practice now?"

Brilliance nodded. "I nearly went to Ambrosia Academy," she said. "I've got a brilliant memory for timetables."

"You nearly went to *Ambrosia Academy*?" Tiptoe gasped. "What happened?"

"It's a long story," Brilliance said. "But it had quite a lot to do with slugs."

Yawning and still wriggling into their clothes, the Naughty Fairies hurried down to the Butterfly Stables. Lord Gallivant was fast asleep on a fern leaf

by the door, with his hair wrapped
carefully around small thistle curlers.

"What's Lord Gallivant doing here?"
asked Ping.

"I think he's guarding the butterflies,"
Brilliance explained.

"He's not very good at it," said Tiptoe.

They stared at the snoozing elf, who
hadn't stirred at the Naughty Fairies'
rather noisy arrival.

To Sesame's relief, Sulphur was
sleeping quietly in the corner of his
stable, his wings folded against his

back. It looked like there hadn't been any more thefts in the night.

Ping unstabled Pong and led him outside, taking care not to tread on Lord Gallivant as they passed. In the brightening dawn light, the Naughty Fairies jumped on to the dragonfly's back. Ping tapped him with her heels, and Pong rose into the sky with his gorgeous wings whirring. Up they flew, over the Hedge and across the Meadow.

Far below, the Naughty Fairies could see the Wood Stump, and the river, and the edge of the Wood. The early sun glinted on the toadstool turrets of Ambrosia Academy as Ping guided Pong down to the low-slung branch of an oak tree which stood nearby. The Naughty Fairies dismounted, and peered over the edge of the branch.

They saw a wide grassy space below them, shielded on two sides by the gnarled roots of the oak tree. Shiny

yellow celandines were beginning to
unfurl their petals as the sunlight crept
into the glade.

"Nice flutterball pitch," said Nettle
admiringly.

"Oooh," said Kelpie in a snooty voice.
"They use *celandines* for goals, do they?
Daisies not good enough for them?"

"Shh," Tiptoe hissed. "I think they're
coming."

A line of pink-dressed fairies began

streaming out of the toadstool turrets,
riding a selection of gorgeously bright
butterflies.

"They've got three Brimstones," said
Sesame in awe. "Look! Red Admirals,
Peacocks – by Nature! Is that a *Clouded
Yellow*? They're *so* rare."

"The pitch is perfect this morning, dear
fairies!" called a sleek, dark-haired elf on
a glossy Painted Lady, who was
zigzagging expertly among the Ambrosia

Academy pupils. "Never in all my days as flutterball coach for the Fairy King himself did I see a better one."

"That elf trained the Fairy *King*?" Brilliance repeated, her eyes round with disbelief. "Isn't he supposed to be the best flutterball player in the whole of the fairy world?"

"I *told* you Ambrosia Academy used a special flutterball coach for the tournament," said Kelpie.

The Naughty Fairies watched as the prettiest Ambrosia Academy fairy rode her Tortoiseshell butterfly up to the elf. She fluffed up her hair a little before she spoke.

"The Fairy King is my uncle, Lord Fandango," she announced with a simpering smile.

"Then you must be Glitter," said Lord Fandango. "Your uncle told me you were a promising little player."

Glitter fluffed up her hair again. "I'm

better than promising. Tremendous and I are the best in the whole school." She patted her butterfly as she spoke.

"Yeah," Brilliance whispered to the others. "The best show-offs."

The Naughty Fairies watched as Lord Fandango released a fluffy little thistle seed. Like a fleet of hungry pink wasps, the Ambrosia Academy fairies watched the seed bob around in the morning breeze and waited for the signal.

"Flutterball!"

"Come on, Gloss!" Glitter called out to a tall fairy riding a magnificent Peacock butterfly. "You and Splendid back me up!"

"But I want to score a goal," Gloss whined.

"Me too!" squeaked a tiny fairy on a rather fat Comma butterfly.

"Me and Tremendous are the goal-scorers, Glee," Glitter said in a lordly voice. "Don't you forget it." And she raced off down the pitch.

"Watch Glitter go," murmured Nettle. "She's really good."

Glitter and Tremendous darted and bounced and spun through the dewy light, fluttering the seed here – there – up – down . . . Within moments, a seed had landed in the gleaming embrace of a shiny yellow celandine. One nil.

"I wish we hadn't come now," said Sesame. "I had no idea they were as good as this."

"Glitter is OK," said Tiptoe, watching the game closely. "But Gloss is only good because she's riding Splendid."

"And Glee is useless," said Nettle. "Her butterfly's going the wrong way."

"Come on, Furbelow!" Glee was squeaking, as her Comma blundered towards the tree roots. "Let'th show them what we're made of!"

Sesame wasn't convinced. "I'm so depressed," she said. "With Lord Fandango coaching them, they'll definitely beat us if we get to the Flutterball Final."

"*Cheats* don't play in the Flutterball Final," Brilliance said. "They've still got all their butterflies, haven't they? So it must be them who've stolen ours!"

"Now what?" Nettle asked.

Brilliance balled her fists. "Let's go get them!"

Down below, a bald-looking dandelion clock lost its last remaining seed.

"Bad idea," said Nettle, catching hold of Brilliance's arm as she prepared to jump off the branch. "We don't have time, and there's only six of us. Let's go back to school and tell Dame Fuddle what we've seen."

"I'm going with Brilliance," said Tiptoe mutinously. "I want Cobalt back."

"Nettle's right," said Sesame, shaking her head. "We'll never find the butterflies on our own."

"Naughty Fairies *never* go to teachers for help," Kelpie thundered. "I can't believe you're suggesting it."

"What about you, Ping?" Brilliance challenged. "Are you coming or going?"

Before Ping could answer, Glitter looked up. Her eyes widened at the sight of the Naughty Fairies high above the flutterball pitch. "Spies!" she shouted, rearing up on Tremendous. "Juniper spies!"

There was a roar of rage from the rest
of the Ambrosia fairies.

"I'm going," said Ping hurriedly,
leaping on to Pong's back. "You?"

For the moment, the Naughty Fairies
forgot their argument. They sprang up
behind Ping. An angry swarm of

Ambrosia Academy fairies chased them
to the edge of the Wood, but Pong's
powerful wings soon put the Naughty
Fairies well out of range – across the
Meadow, over the Hedge and back to
the safety of St Juniper's.

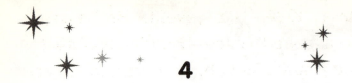

4

The First Clue

All day, the Naughty Fairies argued about what they should do.

Brilliance, Tiptoe and Kelpie wanted to go back to the Wood and find the missing butterflies. Sesame and Nettle were still cautious and wanted to tell Dame Fuddle. And Ping refused to be drawn into the argument. So many petal-paper notes were passed during Fairy Science that Dame Taffeta, the Fairy Science teacher, had to confiscate the fairies' splinter pencils.

At flutterball practice that afternoon, Lord Gallivant put the fairies into teams.

"The heats and the Flutterball Final take place tomorrow," he reminded the class. "Kelpie, Ping, Nettle, Brilliance, Sesame and Tiptoe – I understand that you would like to be in a team together? There were signs of progress at our last practice. We are a little – lower on butterflies than usual, but there are still enough to go round. And with Sulphur on the team, who knows what we might achieve?" Lord Gallivant gave a hopeful smile. "We might produce a result as wondrous as my winning the Midsummer Champion Butterfly Race."

He looked expectantly at the Naughty Fairies, who looked at the floor.

"I don't want to be in a team with *them*," said Kelpie, nodding her head at Nettle and Sesame.

Lord Gallivant swelled. "I have spent a sleepless night guarding . . ."

Sesame snorted.

"A *sleepless* night," Lord Gallivant repeated, "guarding our butterflies to keep them safe for you to fly today –

and you now tell me you don't want to be on a team?"

"Teams should stick together," sniffed Tiptoe.

"*Teams* should listen to each other," Nettle shot back.

"Are you a team or not?" Lord Gallivant asked plaintively.

"No way," Brilliance began.

"Yes," Ping said firmly cutting Brilliance off. "We are."

"Good," said Lord Gallivant, looking relieved. "Your blue team sashes are beside the Butterfly Stable doors. You will play the red team."

The Naughty Fairies stared crossly at Ping as Lord Gallivant moved away.

"Don't look at me like that," said Ping. "The best way to get back at Ambrosia Academy is to beat them in the Flutterball Final and show them that we're above their dirty tricks. And the best way to do *that* is to work as a team."

50

Kelpie gawped at Ping. "But I thought you liked dirty tricks," she said.

"I don't like dirty tricks when we play them against each other," said Ping. "We're the Naughty Fairies. We stick together! Especially when it means beating Ambrosia Academy."

The Naughty Fairies scuffed at the grass with their toes.

"All right," said Kelpie.

"If we have to," said Tiptoe.

"Your enthusiasm bowls me over," said Ping.

"Ping's right," said Nettle. "This is all Ambrosia Academy's fault, and it's like we're blaming each other. That's pretty stupid, isn't it?"

"Come on," pleaded Sesame, who'd already mounted Sulphur. "Let's play flutterball!"

"There's no way I'm riding Snowball again," Brilliance announced. "I shall take Salt."

"Marigold's already got Salt," Tiptoe pointed out, as a brown-haired fairy flew past them on a school Cabbage White.

"Not for long," said Brilliance sweetly.

Flea did a hopeful loop-the-loop and buzzed his wings as hard as he could.

"Not you, Flea," said Kelpie, looking regretful. "We've got to do this properly if we're going to win. And let's face it – you are pretty rubbish."

Flutterball practice went surprisingly well after that. Between them Sesame and Tiptoe scored four times. Kelpie stopped three thistle seeds from landing in the daisies. Ping flew upside down for half the game, which confused the Reds' defence. And because Brilliance was riding a butterfly that wasn't half dead, she and Nettle were able to pass the thistle seed down the pitch as if they were doing it on purpose rather than by mistake.

When Lord Gallivant finally blew his
whistle, the Naughty Fairies had the
highest score of all the St Juniper's

teams. The butterfly-riding teacher was ecstatic.

"I have high hopes," he said jubilantly, as the fairies groomed and stabled the butterflies in the late afternoon light. "At the heats, we must make sure that your team is underestimated." He winked. "That way, we'll have surprise on our side!"

"But that's cheating, Lord Gallivant," Tiptoe said.

"It's not cheating," said Lord Gallivant. "It's tactics."

Word was spreading that the Naughty Fairies' team was the one to watch at the flutterball heats. At supper, fairies crowded around Brilliance and the others to offer flutterball tips. Some tips were weirder than others.

"Shave your butterfly's tummy – it cuts down wind resistance and makes you fly faster . . ."

"Ride a Comma butterfly if you can. The frilly bits on their wings are extra breezy . . ."

"Put cinnamon in your butterflies' nectar. It makes them fart."

"How's that going to help?" asked Tiptoe, giggling.

The fairy who had offered the cinnamon advice winked. "Extra wind power."

"Brilliance!" called Pelly, hurrying over to the Naughty Fairies. "Me, Onion, Vetch and some others are entering a team for the Flutterball Final as well. But don't worry if we meet in the heats. We'll make sure you win the match."

Brilliance was touched. "That's really kind of you, Pelly," she said.

"We'll make sure of it," Pelly said breezily, "because I bet Onion a week's puddings that you win the whole tournament."

"You know," said Sesame, as the Naughty Fairies sat down at their favourite table, "I'm beginning to think we really can win this."

"I hate it when people say that," said Kelpie, taking a big bite out of her sweetpea pasty. "It usually means the opposite is going to happen."

There was a crash at the far end of the Dining Flowerpot. Lord Gallivant was standing at the door, pale-faced and trembling from head to foot.

"My dear Lord Gallivant!" gasped Dame Fuddle from her place at the teachers' table. "Whatever is the matter? You look like you've seen a Human!"

Lord Gallivant cleared his throat. "I'm very sorry to have to tell you," he began, "that in spite of my best efforts – my *very* best efforts to prevent—"

"Get on with it!" called a fairy from the back of the flowerpot.

"The butterflies have gone," Lord Gallivant squeaked. "All of them. Every single one!"

*

Supper was abandoned as the fairies pushed back their chairs and ran to the Butterfly Stables. Sesame was ahead of the crowd by several millisquirts, dragging the others with her.

"Sulphur!" she called, pushing into the stables with her heart hammering in her mouth. "Sulphur!" She gazed in horror at Sulphur's empty stall.

"Even Snowball's gone," Brilliance panted. "How weird is that?"

"The teacher's butterflies too," Kelpie added. "Fraction, Zest, Plankton – every single one of them!"

Tiptoe put her hands to her face. "It's just like Lord Gallivant said!"

"Pong!" Ping screamed.

Pong put his elegant head over his stable door, chewing something grumpily. Ping flung her arms around the dragonfly's slim blue neck and showered him with kisses of relief. And Sesame burst into tears.

As the Naughty Fairies crowded around Sesame to comfort her, the teachers arrived in a swirl of wings and urgent conversation.

"How did this happen?" Dame
Lacewing demanded, as crowds of
excitable fairies ebbed and flowed
around her. "Lord Gallivant?"

"I have been guarding the butterflies
with my life all night and all day, Dame
Lacewing," began Lord Gallivant. "With
my life! I, Gracious Gallivant, the
Midsummer Champion—"

"Stick to the facts, Gracious," Dame

Lacewing interrupted. "When did you leave the stables unattended?"

"Obviously I wasn't in the stables during flutterball practice," said Lord Gallivant after a pause. "But then, neither were the butterflies. During practice, I acquired several grass stains on my new hyacinth-blue hose, and after the fairies went in for supper I briefly – *briefly* – went to my quarters to soak them in soapwort. Grass stains are the worst—"

"*Gracious*," Dame Lacewing snapped.

"I was gone two dandelion seeds," Lord Gallivant said hurriedly. "Five at the most."

"The thieves must have been lying in wait," suggested Dame Honey, from somewhere behind Dame Lacewing. "You don't steal a whole stableful of butterflies without careful planning."

"This is a disaster!" Dame Fuddle said shrilly. "With no butterflies, we must forfeit this year's Flutterball Final! We must send word to Lady Campion at Ambrosia Academy this evening!"

In the chaos which followed this announcement, the Naughty Fairies looked at each other.

"We have to tell Dame Fuddle what we suspect," said Sesame.

"What we *know*," Kelpie corrected, sounding grim.

"Dame Fuddle!" Brilliance called, waving her hands in the air. "Hey! Dame Fuddle! *WE KNOW WHO TOOK THE BUTTERFLIES!*"

The noise in the stables stopped abruptly. Dozens of wide fairy eyes stared in amazement at Brilliance and the others.

"It was Ambrosia Academy," Brilliance began.

"Enough!" Dame Lacewing cut Brilliance off in mid-sentence. "To my office – now."

*

The last time the Naughty Fairies had been in Dame Lacewing's office, it had been to receive one of the worst detentions of their lives. It wasn't surprising, therefore, that the Naughty Fairies were all feeling nervous as they followed the Deputy Head into the small flowerpot study at the edge of the school courtyard.

Dame Lacewing closed the door. "Sit," she said.

The Naughty Fairies sat. So did Dame Lacewing. Pipsqueak, Dame Lacewing's pet rainbow leaf beetle, jumped into the teacher's lap.

"Begin at the beginning," said Dame Lacewing, stroking Pipsqueak.

"Ambrosia Academy have taken the butterflies," said Brilliance.

Dame Lacewing looked intently at Brilliance. "Do you have any proof?"

"We saw Ambrosia Academy practising in the Wood this morning,

Dame Lacewing," said Kelpie, cuddling
Flea. "It didn't look like they'd lost any
of their butterflies, but we've lost all of
ours. Don't you think that's suspicious?"

"The Wood is out of bounds to St
Juniper's fairies," Dame Lacewing
reminded them.

The Naughty Fairies shuffled uneasily
in their seats.

"However," Dame Lacewing said,
"what Kelpie says does sound a little
suspicious."

The Naughty Fairies gawked at Dame Lacewing. They weren't used to being agreed with.

Dame Lacewing steepled her fingers. "A St Juniper's party will visit Ambrosia Academy this evening to forfeit the Flutterball Final," she said.

The Naughty Fairies groaned. And then Dame Lacewing said something very unexpected.

"The rules state that a team of flutterball players must be present when we forfeit the tournament. I would like you six to be that team."

"You want *us* to represent the school?" Brilliance gasped.

Dame Lacewing winced. "With your knowledge of Ambrosia Academy, you will be very – useful," she said.

"You want us to spy while you do the deal?" Ping asked eagerly.

"I want you to keep your eyes open," said Dame Lacewing.

"You want us to spy," said Kelpie, nodding understandingly.

Tears welled up in Sesame's eyes. "I want Sulphur back," she sobbed.

Ping pulled something from her pocket and gave it to Sesame to blow her nose on.

"Urgh!" Sesame spluttered, staring at the floppy black thing in her hands. "What's this? It feels like *skin*!"

"Oops," said Ping. "Sorry. I thought it was my hankie."

An extraordinary expression passed across Dame Lacewing's face. She reached for the object. "Where did you get this, Ping?" she asked.

"Pong was chewing it when we were in the stables just now," said Ping. "Why, what is it?"

"Something impossible," Dame Lacewing murmured, turning the black object over in her hand. She looked up at the fairies. "To the stables!" she said. "We haven't a moment to lose!"

5

Stunts

"I don't understand what's going on," said Brilliance for the hundredth time, as Dame Lacewing pulled open Pong's stable door. "What are we doing here? What was that black thing?"

"How come Pong's not biting Dame Lacewing?" Nettle asked.

The permanently bad-tempered dragonfly was almost purring at Dame Lacewing as the teacher rolled up her sleeves and patted him on the neck.

"Enough questions," said Dame Lacewing. "Help me look."

Ping led Pong out and stood talking to him at the stable door while the Naughty Fairies joined Dame Lacewing on the floor of the dragonfly's stall.

"But what are we looking for?" persisted Brilliance.

"Clues," said Dame Lacewing.

Flea was sniffing something in a dark corner. Kelpie pounced on it. "How about this?" she asked with excitement.

"That's dragonfly poo," said Sesame.

Dame Lacewing sat up on her heels. "Nothing else," she murmured. "Ah well. At least we have the skin." She looked up at the perplexed faces of the Naughty Fairies. "Ping," she said. "Can I borrow Pong for the journey to the Wood?"

"He'll bite you," Ping began.

Dame Lacewing brushed off her gown and held out her hands to Pong. The dragonfly gave a snort of pleasure as he sniffed the teacher's fingers.

"He won't," said Dame Lacewing, and hopped on to the dragonfly's back. Pong stretched his wings, eager to be

off. "Now, are you six coming or not?"

The Naughty Fairies stared at their
teacher with goggling eyes. Then they

leaped on to the dragonfly behind
Dame Lacewing and Pong soared out of
the Butterfly Stables, with Flea doing
his best to keep up.

Pong flew like a greased arrow through
the gusts and eddies of the evening
breeze, and they reached the Wood in
record time.

Dame Lacewing landed Pong expertly
on the branch of a beech tree, and the
Naughty Fairies slid off the dragonfly's
back. Ping tethered Pong to a beech-twig
stem and rubbed his steaming flanks
with a cool leaf.

"Phew," said Kelpie, sliding down to
sit on the pale grey bark. "I need to get
my breath back."

Flea puffed and wheezed into view
and collapsed in a heap next to Kelpie.

"I never knew Pong could fly like
that," said Sesame, in amazement.

"Nor me," sighed Tiptoe.

"Did you, Ping?" Nettle asked.

"Of course I did," Ping said, after a short pause.

Brilliance glanced sideways at Ping. "No you didn't," she said. "You're as surprised as us."

Dame Lacewing clapped her hands. "We use our own wings from here onwards," she said. "Everyone OK with that?" And she launched herself into the dappled woodland air with a whirr.

"Wait!" said Kelpie, grabbing Flea by the scruff of the neck and scrambling to her feet as the others jumped after Dame Lacewing. "Wait for us!"

The Naughty Fairies kept up with difficulty as Dame Lacewing flew on ahead. They swerved and twisted between the trees, ducking to avoid low branches and leaves and trying not to think about the creatures of the Wood who might attack them at any moment.

"Where are we going?" Brilliance
panted at Nettle.

"I don't know," Nettle panted back.
"But this isn't the way to Ambrosia
Academy."

"Urgh," said Kelpie, flying along with
Flea above Brilliance and Nettle.
"What's that stink?"

"We've smelled it before," said
Sesame. "It's marsh gas!"

72

Tiptoe gasped. "Night sprites!" she squeaked. "I think – maybe – Dame Lacewing is looking for *night sprites*!"

They reached a cool, dim glade in the middle of the Wood. Sitting calmly on a great red- and white-spotted toadstool at the foot of a tree, Dame Lacewing was waiting for them.

"Is it true?" Brilliance stuttered as the Naughty Fairies came in to land. "You think night sprites have taken the butterflies, Dame Lacewing?"

"I know it sounds impossible," Dame Lacewing murmured, "but yes."

"I *told* you," said Tiptoe, turning to the others. "I *told* you they existed."

"And the black floppy stuff Pong was chewing?" Nettle asked.

"Batskin," said Dame Lacewing. "Night sprites wear cloaks of batskin. Pong must have bitten a night sprite when it tried to steal him."

"That's my dragonfly," said Ping with pride.

"Do night sprites make a kind of . . . chittering noise, Dame Lacewing?" asked Sesame in a small voice.

Dame Lacewing glanced at her. "Yes. Why do you ask?"

Sesame explained about the noise she'd heard in the stable when Chalky had disappeared.

"If you'd told me that at the start," Dame Lacewing sighed, "we could have nipped all this in the bud."

"OK," said Kelpie. "Let's say night sprites exist. They fly around on moths at night. The butterflies have been disappearing in the day. How does that work exactly?"

"Somehow, the night sprites have discovered life in the daylight," said Dame Lacewing. "They love to fly, you see. It is all they want to do. They can fly by themselves, but flying on moths is better. Now they are awake in the day, and their moths are asleep. What are they going to do?"

"Steal butterflies," said Nettle. It suddenly seemed obvious.

"But why steal ours?" Sesame asked. "What about Ambrosia Academy? Their butterflies are loads better."

"I suspect that butterfly security is tighter at Ambrosia Academy than it is at St Juniper's," said Dame Lacewing dryly. "Ambrosia pupils have some very special butterflies, after all."

In the dimming evening air, there was a flitter of black, yellow and blue. Ping looked stunned, and Kelpie's mouth dropped open.

"There's Sulphur!" Sesame said.

Tiptoe jumped to her feet. "And Cobalt!"

"And more to the point," said Brilliance, sounding dazed, "some real, live night sprites are riding them!"

Dozens of night sprites were whirling

through the air on the backs of
butterflies. They twisted and spun,
twirled and dropped and swooped,
performing impossible mid-air stunts
that made the fairies gasp.

"Chalky's amazing," Brilliance said in
excitement, watching the Large White
perform an incredible three-twist loop
in the air above them. "I never knew he
was so good!"

"Neither did he, I expect," Dame
Lacewing murmured.

In the expert hands of the night sprites, every single butterfly was performing its wings off. Even Snowball could be seen, flying straight up in the air with a whooping night sprite on his back.

Kelpie reluctantly tore her eyes from the display. "So how do we get the butterflies back?" she asked.

Dame Lacewing looked up at the small patch of sky above them. It was beginning to turn a deep, dark blue. "We wait," she said.

Very quickly, the shadows grew so long
and dark that the fairies could barely
see their own hands. Flea fell asleep,
and lay snoozing on the top of the
toadstool. The moon rose above the
trees and cast its hard white light down
into the glade. Reluctantly, the night
sprites flew down to an oak tree in the
middle of the clearing. The Naughty

Fairies watched as they shepherded the
sleepy butterflies into a dark hole in the
heart of the tree.

"We don't have much time," Dame
Lacewing whispered, as the Naughty

Fairies stretched their aching arms, legs and wings. "The night sprites will stable the butterflies before looking for their own supper. While they are occupied, we need to find wood sedge and woolly thistle – quickly!"

Trying to remember what wood sedge and woolly thistle looked like, the fairies hunted around the edge of the glade. Dame Lacewing found a firefly and an acorn-cup cauldron. The Naughty Fairies tipped their ingredients into the cauldron and watched as Dame Lacewing stirred the mixture.

"What are you making, Dame Lacewing?" Nettle asked.

Dame Lacewing poked the firefly. The firefly grumbled, but sparked its tail a little harder, making the mixture bubble and steam in the cauldron. "Something to make the night sprites sleep longer than usual," she said. "Did you see any night-flowering catchfly around here?"

"There's a clump of it at the base of the oak tree," said Tiptoe.

Dame Lacewing raised her eyebrows at the fairies. "You know that night-flowering catchfly . . . ?"

"Is the main food in the night sprites' diet – yes," said Brilliance quickly.

"Thank Nature," said Dame Lacewing. "It seems that you do listen in lessons occasionally." She glanced up at the moon, which was now directly overhead. "We have very little time left to do this," she said. "We need to carry this cauldron to the catchfly."

Nervously the fairies shuffled into the moonlit glade, staggering with the weight of the cauldron. Their shadows looked stark and obvious on the ground. When they reached the crop of night-flowering catchfly, Dame Lacewing handed a slim grass stem to each fairy.

"Dip this in the cauldron," she instructed, "and then dab the mixture

into the catchfly. And mind the sticky stems. Clear?"

The fairies dipped and dabbed, dipped and dabbed until they had done every pale pink catchfly flower. Above them, they heard a chittering noise.

"To the toadstool!" Dame Lacewing ordered, tipping the empty acorn-cup on to its side and making it look as if it had just dropped from the tree. "As fast as you can!"

When they had reached the safety of the toadstool, the fairies glanced back at the oak tree. The night sprites were swarming around the catchfly, nipping off the flowers and chittering among themselves.

"Do you think it's going to work?" asked Kelpie. She poked Flea, who woke up with a start.

"The night sprites should sleep all night and all day, only waking tomorrow evening," said Dame

Lacewing. "We'll find out if it's worked
when we come to collect our butterflies
at dawn tomorrow."

"The others are never going to believe
this," said Brilliance happily.

"Nor are the teachers," said Dame
Lacewing. "Particularly when I give you
all merit points for being so helpful."

"What's a merit point?" asked Ping.

6

The Flutterball Final

When Dame Fuddle stood up at breakfast the following morning and announced that the butterflies had been found, the whole school cheered. Dame Honey, Dame Taffeta, Lord Gallivant and Dame Lacewing had left at dawn to collect the butterflies from the Wood, and a daddy-long-legs had just flown into the Dining Flowerpot with the news that Dame Lacewing's potion had worked and they would all be returning in five dandelion seeds' time. The Flutterball Final was to go ahead as planned that afternoon.

"Into the courtyard – quickly now!" called Dame Fuddle, struggling to make herself heard over the excited chatter in the flowerpot. "Into the courtyard! We must welcome them home!"

Tiptoe looked at her forget-me-not pastry. "But I haven't finished my breakfast" she began.

"Breakfast can wait," said Brilliance, dragging Tiptoe to her feet. "The butterflies are coming home!"

"This is our big moment," said Nettle jubilantly. "We don't want to miss it."

Brilliance and the others had wasted no time telling everyone the part they had played in the drama. Now, as well as being St Juniper's greatest hope for the Flutterball Trophy in more than twenty years, the Naughty Fairies found that they were famous for seeing night sprites as well.

"There were over a hundred," Kelpie told a group of round-eyed young fairies who'd sidled up to hear the story for themselves as the whole school filed outside. "They had the sharpest teeth you've ever seen. One of them even tried to bite me. Of course, my fearless bumblebee soon put a stop to that."

Flea bared his gums in a furry growl.

The little fairies shrieked and scurried away.

As everyone assembled in the courtyard, the Naughty Fairies flew up to the highest flowerpot tower to get a better view. The whole school turned and looked in the direction of the Hedge.

"I can see them!" someone shouted. "They're here!"

The sun crept over the top of the Hedge, dazzling the fairies' eyes. And at last the soft, multicoloured cloud of butterflies swirled into view.

The fairies launched themselves into

the air, eager to help bring the
butterflies in.

"Let me take Salt, Dame Honey . . ."

"You look like you're struggling with
five of them, Lord Gallivant . . ."

"I've got Chalky!
I've got – oh, maybe
not – yup, there we
go . . ."

Tiptoe flew up to
Cobalt with a whoop
and jumped on
his back.

"Sulphur!"
Sesame called,

flinging her arms around her great golden butterfly.

Pelly's ecstatic reunion with her Meadow Brown nearly brought them both crashing down on top of the dandelion clock, while Kelpie and Ping frowned at two Small Whites and tried to work out which was Quince and which was Quartz.

"Well!" Dame Fuddle said, wiping her eyes with a petal hankie. "Well! Come along now, fairies! We just have time to finish our breakfast and head over to the Wood! The flutterball heats are about to begin!"

In the deep green shade of the Wood, fairies gathered along the branches of the oak tree whose roots sheltered the flutterball pitch. St Juniper's purple bunting was strung along one branch, and the soft pink of Ambrosia Academy along another. The flutterball pitch was

looking magnificent, deep and mossy
and dotted with glowing celandine goals.

The Head of Ambrosia Academy, Lady
Campion, stood beside Dame Fuddle in
a knothole in the tree trunk which
overlooked both the branches where the
supporters were sitting and the pitch
itself. Thirty-two flutterball teams were
competing in the early stages of the

tournament. With nearly two hundred competitors riding nearly two hundred butterflies, the air seemed to be filled with colour and the soft beating sound of butterfly wings.

"I'm really getting nervous now," Kelpie muttered, gripping her Small White tightly between her knees. Flea buzzed in anxious circles around Kelpie's head. "Quince feels weird."

"That's because you've got Quartz," said Ping.

"We'll flatten them," said Nettle breezily. "Won't we, Humdinger?" She patted the neck of her neat, sporty Tortoiseshell.

"Just remember everything we practised, won't you?" Sesame pleaded, trying to keep an excitable Sulphur under control.

There was a loud bang and a fizz from Lady Campion's wand.

"Whoa!" Brilliance struggled to stay

on Chalky's back as the Large White
did a sudden sideways loop in fright.

Competitors and supporters turned to
face the knothole in the oak trunk.

"Ambrosia Academy," said Lady
Campion in a grand voice.

The Ambrosia fairies cheered.

"St Juniper's!" said Dame Fuddle.

The St Juniper's fairies cheered
louder.

"You all know the rules," declared

Lady Campion, adjusting her sparkly spectacles on the end of her nose. "The first team to win three goals gets through to the next stage."

There were more cheers.

"If you lose or forfeit a match, you are out of the competition," Lady Campion continued.

Shouts of "You're rubbish, Juniper!" and "We'll fly you into the ground, Ambrosia!" followed this.

"When we have two teams left, the Flutterball Final itself will commence,"

Lady Campion finished. "On your wings . . ."

"Get set!" said Dame Fuddle, nearly falling out of the knothole in her excitement.

"FLUTTERBALL!" shouted the two head teachers together.

"FLUTTERBALL!" bellowed nearly two hundred voices back – and sixteen flutterball matches began all at once.

Even the best flutterball pitches struggle to hold sixteen matches all at the same

time. On the mossy, celandine-dotted perfection of the Ambrosia Academy pitch, fairies crashed into each other, wings got bent, butterflies got bruised and thistle seeds got ripped to shreds. Four teams declared themselves out on account of injuries. Three matches collapsed into fist fights as the fairies accused each other of cheating. Six referees were knocked out cold and two retired in tears.

Soon, the thirty-two teams had been whittled down to sixteen. Then eight. The pitch started to look empty and the celandine goals could be seen more clearly, shining golden against the soft green moss.

"Just the semi-final to go," panted Sesame, swooping down to join Brilliance and the others after winning a difficult match against a team of Ambrosia fairies riding Commas. "And then we're in the Final!"

"The Final!" cheered the Naughty Fairies, adjusting their blue team sashes. It seemed impossible but true. Their butterflies hadn't forgotten the tricks they'd learned from the night sprites, and had flown like the wind.

"Semi-finalists!" shouted Lord Fandango. "On your wings! Get set! Flutterball!"

"I don't believe it," Nettle gasped. "We're playing Pelly's team!"

Sure enough, Pelly and fellow team-mates Onion, Vetch, Marigold, Tinkle and Teazel were grinning at them.

The teams winked at each other.

"Ouch," Pelly shouted. She dramatically clutched her shin. "I forfeit the match!"

"We all forfeit the match!" shouted her team-mates.

Lady Campion frowned. "Very well," she said. "The winners are the Blues. The Final will take place in five dandelion seeds' time!"

Both branches of supporters erupted with cheers and catcalls as the Naughty Fairies hugged Pelly and her team-mates. They were through!

Brilliance suddenly felt a powerful breeze at her back.

"Hello, Not-So-Brilliance," smirked Glitter. Tremendous fluttered his fabulous Tortoiseshell wings again, nearly blowing

Brilliance off Chalky's back. "Lovely Cabbage White you've got there."

"Oh no," Tiptoe groaned.

"Are you ready for total humiliation?" purred Glitter, tweaking her pale pink team sash.

"Yes," said Brilliance in defiance. "Yours."

Flea hid behind Kelpie.

"I'm glad it's you," Kelpie hissed, reaching out to pet her bee comfortingly on the head. "We've got an old score to settle."

"*We'll* be the ones scoring around here," smirked Gloss. She dug her

heels into Splendid's sides and the Peacock butterfly zoomed into position.

The red-haired referee elf looked worried as the two flutterball teams glared ferociously at each other across the mossy pitch.

"This will be a clean match," he began.

"Get on with it, ref," Kelpie snarled.

"Very well then. On your wings, get set – oof . . ."

"Not *oof*," Tiptoe reminded the referee as Kelpie charged him out of the way. *"Flutterball."*

"Flutterball!" bellowed Glitter and her team-mates.

"Flutterball!" the Naughty Fairies bellowed back.

The thistle seed was lost in an instant as both teams kicked their butterflies and zoomed in.

"Where is it?" Kelpie yelled, staring around. "I can't see it!"

"Behind you!" roared the crowd.

"Above you!"

Sesame and Tiptoe pounced and fluttered the thistle seed down the pitch. But moments later, Gloss had puffed it out of their reach and was racing in the opposite direction.

"I've got it, Gloth! I've got it!" squeaked Glee, urging her butterfly forward.

"Yoo hoo," said Ping, flying upside down above Glee's head.

Glee looked up. "Huh?"

Ping swung Quartz into a somersault and took control of the thistle seed. The

St Juniper's supporters yelled their approval as she sped down the pitch and passed the seed to Brilliance, who flipped it into a celandine.

Half the oak tree shook with cheers. *"Gooooal!"*

"Nooo!" shouted the other half.

But the Naughty Fairies' triumph was short. Ambrosia Academy scored the next goal, and the one after that. The score was 2-1. Ambrosia Academy only needed one more goal to win the trophy.

"Who's laughing now?" sang the Ambrosia Academy fairies.

"We've got to pull this together, team!" Brilliance shouted, swooping after the fluttering seed and barging Glitter out of the way. "We need two more goals!"

Kelpie and Ping fought off Ambrosia Academy's attempts to steal the thistle seed while Brilliance and Tiptoe fluttered it towards the nearest celandine. A gust of wind suddenly picked up the seed and pushed it down to the ground, out of the Naughty Fairies' reach. Glitter swept after it, her head down and Tremendous's wings angled for maximum speed.

"No!" Tiptoe shouted in dismay.

"Yes!" shouted Brilliance as the wind pushed the thistle seed into the celandine before Glitter had reached it. "Goal! Just one more, team! Naughty Fairies for ever!"

The sun was setting, and a wide stripe of blazing yellow sunshine made the shiny celandine goals look like they were on fire. A hush fell on the glade as the players squinted through the light for the thistle seed one last time.

Suddenly, the seed was in front of Sesame, fluffy and golden. Without thinking, Sesame drove her heels into Sulphur's sides and pelted after it. The crowds, the trees and the glade faded

away. The only thing Sesame could see
was the seed. She angled the
Brimstone's wings – puffed the seed
towards a celandine so bright and sunlit

that it hurt to look at it – and . . .

"GOOOOOOAAAAAALLLLL!"

The whistle blew, and the glade
erupted. Ambrosia Academy could only
stand and watch as the Naughty Fairies
were mobbed by the crowd.

"I think we just won," Tiptoe
squeaked, before disappearing beneath
a pile of celebrating St Juniper fans.

"We won, we won, we won!" Sesame
yelled in delight.

"I always knew we would," grinned
Ping, and high-fived Nettle.

Kelpie jumped off Quartz, fought
through the crowd and hurled herself at
an ecstatic Flea. They tumbled together
in a whirling black and yellow hug.

"Brilliant," Brilliance sighed, as she
raised her hand and waved regally to
the cheering crowd. "Totally, utterly,
brilliantly brilliant."

Around the night-tinged edges of the
glade, several flittering black figures

peeped through the branches at the
brightly coloured crowd. Then, quietly
chittering at each other, they melted
back into the darkness.